P9-DDN-191

PERFECT SHADOW

By Brent Weeks

Perfect Shadow

THE NIGHT ANGEL TRILOGY

The Way of Shadows
Shadow's Edge
Beyond the Shadows

Night Angel (Omnibus)

THE LIGHTBRINGER SERIES

The Black Prism
The Blinding Knife
The Broken Eye
The Blood Mirror
The Burning White (Summer 2018)

PERFECT SHADOW

BRENT WEEKS

www.orbitbooks.net

This book is a work of fiction. Names, characters, places, and incidents are the product of the author's imagination or are used fictitiously. Any resemblance to actual events, locales, or persons, living or dead, is coincidental.

Author photograph by Travis Johnson Photography
Cover design by Lauren Panepinto
Cover photo by Gene Mollica

Orbit
Hachette Book Group
1290 Avenue of the Americas
New York, NY 10104
orbitbooks.net

Perfect Shadow: A Night Angel Novella originally published in ebook in 2011 by Orbit
"I, Night Angel" originally self-published in 2014
First Hardcover Edition: November 2017

Orbit is an imprint of Hachette Book Group.
The Orbit name and logo are trademarks of Little, Brown Book Group Limited.

The publisher is not responsible for websites (or their content) that are not owned by the publisher.

Library of Congress Control Number: 2017948319

ISBNs: 978-0-316-47740-6 (hardcover), 978-0-316-47738-3 (ebook), 978-0-316-48087-1 (Barnes & Noble Signed Edition)

Printed in the United States of America

LSC-C

10 9 8 7 6 5 4 3 2 1

This one's for Chelsea Crawford.
I bet they have the best stories there.

Perfect Shadow

A Night Angel Novella

Chateau Shayon is supposed to be impregnable. I love it when they say that. Crushing a bare rock just offshore with their weight, the chateau's sheer walls ring the entire island, actually overhanging the waters of Lac Shayon in places.

This was to be my first kill for hire. It's good to start with the impossible. Make a name for myself. Enter with a splash.

I emerged from the water with little more than a ripple. The walls loomed before me, above me. There were no shallows to stand in. In those few places where there once had been, some lord or another had sent masons to chip away rock to a depth of three paces below water. I was naked to the waist, skin smeared with fat and ashes for insulation and invisibility. Clothes would have simply filled with water, slowed me down.

As it was, I was bleeding from a slash along one cheek and several cuts along my forearms. Defensive wounds. I didn't want to stay in that water any longer than I had to. There were more of those damned things out there.

But I waited. Clung to the rocks, buffeted by the waves, studying the wall. There were easier ways to do this, of course. The *ka'kari* could make most anything easy. Except those things that it makes damn near impossible.

~You don't want to do this, Acaelus. Murder for hire? You?~

None of that. That's not my name. Hasn't been for a long time.

The overhang of the walls was lined with machicolations for rocks, murder holes for arrows, and spouts for jellied fire. I could see two sentries above me in mail and wool, chatting, checking the lake from time to time. It was a clear night, lit by a full moon. Not a night that required much vigilance. I saw six other men atop the wall, eight. Far enough away that I shouldn't have been able to see them in the darkness.

But darkness welcomes my eyes. It was one way I couldn't help but use the ka'kari. It forever altered how I see.

Almost every window of the chateau was shuttered against the cold night breeze. I wasn't looking for an open window, though. Every window was barred, and every iron bar was in good condition. There were no balconies over the picturesque lake; that would only give grapnels a place to hook. This chateau had been built for defense, and not by fools.

A simple assassin would fail.

Only on the third story did the windows of the chateau—again barred with stout iron—glow with cheery firelight, shutters thrown open. That would be the great hall, where Baron Rikku was entertaining his vassals. Baron Rikku was a proud man. Proud of his parties. Proud of the fine Sethi wines he served. Proud of his ornaments, his silks, his art. Proud of his piety. Proud of seizing this little island chateau from its previous owner.

Unfortunately, the previous owner of the island hadn't actually owned the island. He'd merely been holding it for another. One who wished to keep her ownership anonymous. One who wasn't impressed by the baron. One who wouldn't forgive him for his ignorance, or his theft.

But that's what sucks about running an underworld, isn't it? Tell people what you own, and you invite attacks from those strong enough to challenge you; don't tell people what you own, and you won't dissuade those who fear you.

Right, poor Sa'kagé, you really get the ass-end of life.

I checked the position of the moon, judging how far it had moved since I'd entered the water on the other side of the lake, some two thousand paces distant. The baron would retire from the party, make love with his wife in her chambers or with one of her ladies or a maid in a side room he kept for the purpose, and then use the lords' privy before retiring to his own chambers on the top floor.

Classic defensive weaknesses of any fortification: how shit comes in and how shit goes out. Here, the garderobe overhung the water, so I was able to find the privies by their smell. The chute was narrow, probably as much to minimize how much wind blew up on your nethers as for defense. The chute didn't start until five paces above the water, and its narrowness meant every surface was slick with effluents. With slimy fresh diarrhea caked over the top of crumbly feces dried and aged into soil, there was no telling where the cracks in the rock were.

I glanced up, saw that none of the guards were looking, and then something caught my eye behind me: a shadow in the waters.

More than one. Dozens. Fucking fanged fish. Undeniably stupid, but I'd heard they could smell blood for a league. Apparently I should have believed it.

With a surge of my Talent, I shot out of the

water. I stabbed fingers and bare toes into the shit-slick walls, pushed off, twisted, leapt for the inside wall of the chute, twisted, and had both my left hand and left foot betrayed by bad holds.

I fell, fingers clawing at the walls, toes scratching, tearing off toenails, finally stopped. I gave myself a few deep breaths and then launched upward again with magic-augmented strength. This time, I bounced lightly from one side to the other.

Almost at the top, I found the remains of a grate. It must have been installed hundreds of years ago, because the iron was corroded to little more than nubs sticking out of each wall. Too much trouble to replace, apparently, or too gross. Now it made good footholds for the very kind of man it had originally been intended to keep out.

The problem with a place like Chateau Shayon wasn't that it had a weakness. Every castle has weaknesses. The problem was that when you steal a chateau from Gwinvere Kirena, you have an enemy who knows your weaknesses exhaustively.

Most assassins wouldn't try the garderobe. Not because they're squeamish, but because there's always a security grate. Honestly, if I'd thought it was *still* one—well, maybe I'd have chosen a cleaner path to a dirtier kill.

Balancing on the stubs of the grate, ignoring my bleeding toes, I drew a plane saw. The privies were a simple board: oak, with three holes in it. Three so you and two friends can drop mud together, I guess. Call me unsociable, but no thanks. Regardless, if Gwinvere's intelligence were still accurate, the board was fitted with a lock and bolted down. No one even had the key to that lock anymore. I picked the middle hole, setting the plane saw to work inscribing a circle slightly larger than the current one.

~This goes against everything you've lived for. Gaelan, this isn't you.~

No, this isn't Gaelan. There is no Gaelan. I'm nameless.

No one came to use the lords' privies in the time I was there. Lucky. It does happen. That's the thing. If you're prepared to get shit on and do your work anyway, sometimes you get lucky. Over the distant sounds of laughter and carousing—*You will be alone. You will be separate. Always.*—I listened for footsteps.

None. I scraped some feces off the wall next to my head, reached my hand up through the right side privy-hole, and plopped the feces on the seat. I pulled an empty leather winebag, smaller than my clenched fist, from where it was rolled flat under my belt. I opened it, balanced somewhat precariously on the grate-stubs, and pissed in the bag.

Then I poured the urine liberally around the left-side privy's seat.

I'd barely finished when the door banged open. The baron. He was preceded by a soldier carrying a lantern.

The soldier searched the room for intruders, though there wasn't much searching to do. The room was bare rock with a low ceiling and only the one entrance. Apparently the baron was nervous.

The soldier walked toward the privies. I

pressed myself against one wall and drew the shadows around me. It wasn't anything like invisibility, but it helped. And the lantern's light was diffuse—that's the problem of using a lantern to look straight down: the base gets in the way. The man's head appeared, but he was light-blind.

"Quickly, would you?" the baron said. "I'm going to die of a burst bladder here."

No, you're not.

The light above steadied as the soldier put it on a hook, and then the door closed.

A moment later, I heard the baron swear, mumbling to himself, "...swine. Can't even piss without missing the hole...whoreson Alitaerans." There was a rustle of clothing as he dropped his trousers, and his ass blocked out the light over the middle privy. "...wines from Seth, chef from the best Modaini...Probably shat on the edge on purpose."

He was a lean man, but the wood groaned slightly where I'd incised the larger circle. But it didn't give way. Not yet.

I let him finish his business. Never say I'm not a gentleman.

I was once the avatar of retribution. Now I just try to be polite.

A moment later, the baron disappeared down the privy without a trace. When his soldiers grew suspicious and checked, he was simply gone. You'll forgive me if I don't dwell on the details. You see, this isn't the tale of Baron Rikku's death. It's the tale of mine.

But afford me a moment for my professional pride and let me say this: in the Chateau Shayon, no one ever again shat unworried.

"What I don't understand is why you came to Cenaria. There's nothing here. It's a hole," Yvor Vas says. He's a skinny, freckled redhead who—improbably enough—hails from Ladesh.

"They don't know me here," I say. I'm drinking ale. He's drinking ootai—all Ladeshians are addicted to the bitter drink, apparently even the redheaded ones—in a little safe house I'd purchased in the Warrens on the edge of swampland. This conversation is too dangerous to risk it being overheard. "In the last fifty years, I've become famous in most of the great nations. There've been so many wars, and I always seem to end up in the middle of them."

He says, "You were Vin Craysin in eastern Alitaera, Tal Drakkan in Seth, Gorrum Quesh in Modai, and Pips McClawski in western Alitaera?" Trying to impress.

"You know I found a collector who had Pips's dice in Aenu? And no, I wasn't Gorrum Quesh, though I fought with him for a time. You Society folk, always so curious." I wasn't Vin Craysin either, but I don't like to reveal all of my cards, even when it doesn't matter.

"The Society of the Second Sun would like to be an asset for you, Master Starfire. Allies who will help you, regardless of your circumstances. Think of it!"

"I have," I say. I pause, deep in thought. "And I want to tell you everything."

His eyes light up.

Everyone thinks they're special. It's what makes lying so easy.

"Gaelan Starfire! What an honor. Thank you for agreeing to meet me." Gwinvere Kirena owned the kind of beauty that made a man remember being twelve and unable to speak in the presence of a girl. Gaelan had met great beauties before. The truth was, most of the encounters left him convinced that people were idiots. Great beauties and stunningly handsome men were accorded virtues: people found them funnier, smarter, more insightful than they actually were.

Conversely, he'd met women reputed to be great beauties who'd been merely attractive but with great confidence, charm, or vivacity. Gwinvere Kirena might be the former, but she definitely wasn't the latter. He'd heard her described as "the courtesan of the age." She was maintained by many men, owned by none. And this, at perhaps thirty years old.

His pause had to have been obvious, but Gaelan guessed Gwinvere was used to men finding lead in their tongues—and iron in their… elsewhere. "It's not my usual kind of gathering, but you roused my curiosity," Gaelan said.

He was looking at her eyes, not her generous cleavage, as he said "roused." A beauty, much less a courtesan, would be accustomed to men's advances, from the most vulgar to the most genteel. Her eyes gave away nothing. Either she'd missed it, didn't care, or she chose not to give anything away.

"Are you enjoying the party?" she asked.

Gaelan's back stiffened. It was a masque, held in some absent lord's rented manse. He hadn't seen such degeneracy since the waning days of the first Alitaeran Empire. He was reasonably handsome and very athletic, but no less than three women had *groped* him in the time between his coming through the front door and coming to this study. He'd even recognized one of them—the young wife of an earl, her face covered with a swan mask, and not much else covered at all. She'd laughed and addressed her friends by name, apparently not concerned about being identified. Gaelan hadn't seen anyone actually copulating, but the night was young.

"It's been an education," he said.

Gwinvere Kirena herself had opted for a thin, high-collared, shockingly red dress perfectly cut to show every curve. She was bedecked with narrow gold chains, crossing between her breasts, bound with a padlock that hung in front of her hips. On a ribbon choker around her neck, she wore a little golden key. Some tailor's fantasy of a Khalidoran harem girl, complete with chastity belt.

"I held it for you," she said.

"I've never had anyone hold an orgy for me," he said honestly. Not in 680 years.

She chuckled. "I was testing your rectitude," she said. A slight pause before *rectitude.* Setting him up for the double entendre, if he wished. Allowing him to pursue her, if he wished.

But what she meant was that she was seeing if Gaelan Starfire would turn around and leave such a party before he even met her, or if he would tolerate debauchery. What kind of a man is Gaelan Starfire? she was asking.

A good test, devised by an incisive mind.

"Say your piece. You didn't invite me here for my wit, or my cock."

Her eyes widened for a moment; then a smile curved her full, rouged lips. She lay back against her divan. "I hadn't *thought* I had," she said. "You're making me reconsider."

He folded his hands behind his back, legs apart, bearing military.

Her eyes played over his figure. She said, "Gaelan Starfire, farmer from nowhere turned hero of the Ceuran Campaigns, master of the longbow, master of the warhammer. Single-handedly freed a hundred of his imprisoned comrades. Five times refused promotions. Held the ridge at the Battle of Blood Grass all by himself. Suspected of being Talented, but twice refused to be examined by the Sisters. Quarreled bitterly with his Alitaeran commander, and then left suddenly. Recently accused of murder and hunted by armies from Alitaera and Ceura both."

"Stories. Half true at best. They bore me."

"The Alitaeran commander turned up dead a month later," she said.

"Really?" he said, too slowly. How could she know that? "Serves that bastard right."

"When he recruited you, he promised you vengeance on the Ceurans, didn't he." It wasn't a question. "Then he took *their* bribe to call off the campaign." Again, not a question.

"So you think I'm a murderer. You want me as an assassin?" Gaelan asked. "What? Some pretty rival slight you? A lover spurn you?"

He intended her to take offense. Wanted to see her angry.

She smiled indulgently. Full lips, beautiful smile, light in her eyes at being challenged. Enjoying being challenged. "I'm Sa'kagé, Gaelan."

"Of course you are." The underworld lords, the Sa'kagé, ran all of the significant crime in the city under the watchful eye of their ruling Nine, who were in turn watched by a Shinga, whose power would make kings jealous. One of those Nine ran all of the prostitution in Cenaria. That man, the Master of Pleasures, wouldn't let a beautiful woman like Gwinvere Kirena operate independently. So maybe that was it. Maybe she wanted out.

"I wasn't finished." She stood, walked over to check the lock on the door. He noticed that the gold chains actually disappeared into a cut in her dress, apparently wrapping beneath her body to emerge at her bare back, which it covered in an artful golden lattice of bondage. Her beauty made his breath catch and his mind slow, and he needed his mind with this one. "I'm one of the Nine," she said. "The Mistress of Pleasures."

It was not a secret to be casually shared. “Young to be—”

“I have a plan, and I need you for it.”

He thought about it. Gaelan Starfire was supposed to be forty-five years old now, and he looked at least a decade younger. Gaelan was famous, but he had few real friends, and many enemies. Maybe it was time to move on, let that name die. There were worse things than to ally yourself with a beautiful, intelligent woman.

“What’s your plan?” he asked.

She turned. “There’ll be time for that. First, we need to take care of something.” She extended her hand. He took what was in it.

It was the golden key she’d been wearing on her choker.

He cocked an eyebrow, trying to ignore the shock running to his loins. Having the body of a young man meant having the reactions of a young man, too. “Why?” he asked.

“Because if we don’t fuck tonight, you might fall in love with me. But if we do, you’ll probably still desire me—in fact, I'll consider it a professional failure if you don't; this *is* my work, after all—but you'll never trust me. You'll know that I'll do the same with any other man who catches my fancy. It'll make things simpler."

~An honest whore. A rare woman in a dozen ways. She's poisoning the well and telling you, Acaelus. Is that really what you want?~

"And you?" he asked her. Are you in no danger of loving me?

She came close, slowly, gently, into his arms. The scent of fine perfume and the insidious softness of silk and skin. Cold gold chains on his skin and a warm breath in his ear. "I intend to enjoy my work tonight."

In their little farmhouse, Gaelan held his wife's bare ass, balanced on the edge of a table he'd made himself. She held his shoulder and the back of his head, her pupils wide, hips trembling against him with the aftershocks of their lovemaking.

She dug her fingernails into his shoulder painfully, playfully. “You know Ali could be home any minute.” But her eyes were shining, and she didn’t uncross her ankles from behind his butt, didn’t push him away.

“There’s worse things than a girl finding out her father still finds her mother irresistible.”

She grinned, and squeezed him with her thighs.

“Your smile is a century of solace,” he told her, trying to lock her face in his memory. She was beautiful, hair atumble, face flushed with sex and joy. Content and content with him. It was a treasure. She would grow old, die, and he would remain, young, immortal, following the directives of a long-dead king. A long-dead friend.

“Flattery already got you everything you’re going to get,” she said.

He laughed and pinched her ass.

She swatted his hand, eyes aglow.

"Why is all our happiness doomed?" he asked her.

She looked into his eyes, loving, gentle. "You are a cipher, my lord."

"No, I was Samon Cipher six lives ago," he said, winking, trying to salvage the moment.

"Mother!" a girl's voice called out, right outside the door to their little cottage.

Gaelan pulled back, hiked his trousers up, yanked his belt tight, and slapped at his hair, trying to flatten it. Seraene hopped off the table, smoothing her skirts, grabbing a rag so she could pretend to be cleaning.

The door opened and Alinaea stepped in, carrying a basket of fresh-picked herbs in one hand and the day's eggs in the other. If she'd been much older, he and Seraene would have been totally caught. The smell in the cottage wasn't exactly subtle, and neither was the sex flush visible on Seraene's chest, or the stubble-burn from his whiskers in the bit of cleavage her dress showed. But Alinaea was eight years old. Innocent. She was the light of Gaelan's eyes.

"Da," she said, serious, cocking her head to one side. "I've decided. I'm old enough now for a little brother."

Gaelan looked over at Seraene. She was beaming. She put her hand on her belly.

"This? This is how you tell me?!" he demanded.

She laughed.

By all the gods that were and all the gods that had never been, how he missed Seraene's laugh.

The pleasures rolled over Gaelan—and passed, leaving him cold. Gwinvere was astride him, clad only in those delicate golden chains. She stopped once he finished, not having climaxed herself. This was business for her, after all, not pleasure. But she didn't get off him.

She stared at him, her hair tussled, figure

magnificent, letting him bask in her radiance, letting him store up the image of a woman of her supernal beauty, making love with him. She leaned over him, and something like pity flashed through her eyes.

"You are a god clad in flesh, Gaelan Starfire, and you're more fragile than you know. Be ware."

She lay on his chest and tucked her head into his shoulder, but just for a moment. The room was cool, and he was warm; maybe she was just appreciating that physical warmth and nothing more. She got up almost immediately. She began dressing, and he knew with a cynical twinge that she must have practiced dressing like this in a looking glass, because every move was graceful. She wasn't just a whore; she was an artist, and this last impression he would carry of her was as important to her as the first.

"I want to fuck again," he said. "Now." This time he wouldn't think of Seraene. Gwinvere was a wonder. He should appreciate her. He should please her.

"So do I, but I've three other men to bed before dawn, a fourth if he's kind."

"Was I your first—" He cut off. Ridiculous question. He couldn't believe he'd asked it. He didn't know where it had come from.

"Yes, Gaelan, I was a virgin until just now," she said flatly.

"I meant of the night," he said in a rush, flustered. "Never you mind. Stupid question."

She looked at him, hesitated. "You're magnificent. Distracted, but magnificent. Let's fuck tomorrow, after I finish dinner with the ambassador. Then you can tell me if you accept my business proposal."

Proposal? She hadn't even asked for anything yet.

A few minutes later, Gaelan pushed through a fog of riotweed, through which he saw the vague outlines of the debauched. Silent servants, costumed uniformly as black horses with blinkered eyes, tended to those who'd overindulged, carrying off those who were ill, tucking pillows under the heads of the unconscious, and covering nude bodies with blankets. The earl's wife, now wearing nothing but her swan mask and one silk stocking, ran toward Gaelan squealing, pursued by two lascivious lords whose masks had fallen off.

Before she could run into him, or look to him for protection that she really didn't want, Gaelan ducked into a noisy side room. Musicians were sitting behind an opaque curtain, muscling out a bastardized version of a Haranese tribal beat. Two older lords smoking ornate bowls of riotweed were watching a third lord as he danced with a woman. Gwinvere.

The big ape had his fist wrapped around Gwinvere's slender neck. She ground into him sinuously, her back to him, running her hands down his hips.

She saw Gaelan, missed one beat, and then continued dancing. As she took fistfuls of the young lord's trousers and pulled him tight against her ass, she didn't look away.

Gaelan did. He ducked out into the party, and then out into the night.

He was followed.

Whoever was following Gaelan, he was good. Very good. But Gaelan had options. The hunted always has options, and Gaelan's futures spun out as simply as the different men he'd been over the last 680 years. Different men, different choices, different futures, splitting:

As a young man, the man he'd been born, as Prince Acaelus Thorne, he identified a choke point that even a careful pursuer would have to pass through lest he lose his quarry. Acaelus hid behind the first good corner and waited. He gathered his Talent, ready to overwhelm his pursuer, capture him, hit him a few times to find out who had sent him. He waited—

No, no, that wasn't true. Prince Acaelus hadn't had even that much subtlety.

Hiding? Acaelus? Ha!

No, Acaelus turned as soon as he became aware of his pursuer. Stopped in the open street.

"I know you're there! Come out! If you want a fight, I'll give it to you. If you want to know where I'm bound, come ask. I am crown prince of the dead kingdom of Trayethell, and I'll not have this mummery. Face me!"

The spy fled. Acaelus heard the skittering of scattering gravel, zeroed in on the sound, and ran in pursuit. His Talent lent strength to his muscles. He ran faster. He drew his sword, rounded a corner that was too sharp for the speed he was running.

He leapt, pushed off a wall, blasted the spy off his feet. The man tumbled head over heels, lay still.

Acaelus approached the spy. The little man lay on his back, hooded and cloaked.

At the last second, the spy convulsed. Two daggers flew through the air, straight for Acaelus.

With preternatural speed, Acaelus's blade swatted left, right, riposte. The daggers were batted aside and his sword was in the spy's heart before he had a second thought.

. . . And he learned nothing.

Not that Acaelus had ever had second thoughts. Not that he would doubt his own actions.

No, Acaelus had been a noble fool. His way would be a disaster. Rejected.

Dehvirahaman Bruhmaeziwakazari would have—no, the Ymmuri stalker was a canny hunter, but he would have never come into a city. His leather pouches and camouflage cloaks had been perfect for his natural environs, but here clothes mattered in a different way. Rejected.

Rebus Nimble. There was a life that might have had some success here. Rebus was a sneak thief turned folk hero for making several hundred pounds of a corrupt king's gold rain in the streets in every market in town simultaneously.

Rebus would have headed to the rough side of town. Here, the west side, the Warrens.

Rebus took a circuitous route, as if careful of being followed but not aware that he actually was. Spies always like to think they're good.

If the spy were simply some lord's or lady's lackey, he'd get nervous and break off his pursuit as Rebus crossed the Vanden Bridge into the Warrens. He didn't. That meant the spy had been sent by someone formidable. Rebus abandoned his apparent caution once he reached the slums, walking quickly, which always made his limp more pronounced.

He limped down an alley. Took a left, a right, two lefts, followed a street so narrow his outstretched hands could touch both slumping walls to either side. And after three hundred paces with no outlet, reached a dead end. Dammit. These weren't the slums of Borami, where he knew every bolt-hole. In fact, he might have just played right into his hunter's hands.

He turned. The spy stood there, dual long-knives drawn. So, not a spy, an assassin. And two archers who looked like they knew what they were doing stood on either side of him.

"Rebus *Nimble*," the assassin said, lifting his chin toward Rebus's twisted right foot. "Irony?"

"Older I get, the more I hate irony. But I was young once. I made it up when I started serious body magic. Making your arms and legs longer makes you clumsy as all hell for a while. I was hoping to make the name ironic eventually."

"I guess we'll see how that turned out."

Arrows streaked forward, burning holes in the night.

More blood, more death, and no more answers.

No, Rebus's instincts were all wrong. Besides, in his fine clothes, Gaelan might get jumped by robbers in the Warrens before he even had a chance to get cornered by an assassin. Rejected.

So, Gaelan, those men you've been are no help to you. What will the dirt-farmer-turned-

war-hero do? Who will you be now? Who will you be next?

Gaelan wouldn't let the spy dictate to him. He was done with that. He simply didn't care. Truth was, Gaelan—the Gaelan he had envisioned when he discarded his previous life as Tal Drakkan, the Gaelan he had been for the last twenty-five years—was plain and direct. More like Acaelus. Until the end. Now that Gaelan was dripping away, like a wax mask exposed to fire. And he wasn't sure who was emerging. Or what.

He walked to his inn by the most direct route. There was only one good place for an assassin to attack him—if assassin he was. Gaelan walked through it. No attack. He went straight to his room, bearing a lantern that the sleepy-eyed porter handed him. He opened the door into the darkness of his room, stepped inside, and blew out the lantern.

The garish light of the lantern should have spoiled the night vision of any assassin, if one waited in his room. And the sudden darkness should leave him blind.

But Gaelan wasn't blind. The shadows had welcomed his eyes since he bonded the ka'kari. No one was in his room. His magical seals on the windows remained.

He went to bed, not having confronted anyone, not having killed anyone. It was the right move. Patience was a lesson immortality should have taught him long ago.

Wisdom is boring.

"You're the best I've ever had," Gaelan said, after their fourth round of lovemaking.

"I get that a lot," Gwinvere said. Teasing, but keeping her distance, her professionalism. They lay together in her bedchamber, naked, her head on his chest.

Not from men who are 680 years old.

He tweaked her nipple in punishment. She laughed, and he joined her.

"Someone followed me here," Gaelan said. "One of your people?"

A half second of hesitation, a bit of tension in her body against him. A yes. But she didn't try to lie. "He followed you last night, too. I wanted to see if you'd report to anyone that I was trying to hire you."

"Mm-hmm. So what you want me to do is treasonous. And all you know is that I don't have to report daily. Maybe I'm just on a long leash." So he had done the right thing. Killing a servant of the Nine mightn't have been the best way to start in a new city.

She traced designs idly on his chest, weighing her words. Finally, she said, "You're a risk I'll take. You've heard of wetboys?"

"Magic-using assassins?"

"There's only a limited number of them at any one time. No one ever knows how many. But they all swear a magically binding oath of fealty to the Shinga. They can't harm him or take contracts without his approval. Right now, there are only five wetboys. I want you to kill four of them."

"And the fifth?"

"Will train you. He was the man who followed you last night and today. Ben Wrable."

"Scarred Wrable?" Gaelan had heard the name, but not much else.

"He's got a few... quirks."

There was only one reason you'd get rid of all the Shinga's assassins if you were already on the Nine. "And after I kill these wetboys? You want me to kill the Nine as well? The Shinga?"

She sat up, and despite his satiety, he couldn't help but look at her body first, then her eyes. "No," she said. "I'm taking care of them in other ways."

"So you become Shinga, and I become a wetboy who hasn't sworn the oath of obedience to you. After using me, won't you find me too dangerous to keep around?"

A pause. "You're a clear thinker, Gaelan Starfire. I like that. Most men would have expressed some shock at being asked to kill. Or some doubt about a woman running the Sa'kagé."

I've known Irenaea Blochwei and Ihel Nooran. No doubts. "So?" he said instead.

"You'll look into my history, of course. See how I've treated prostitutes who retire. Find out how I treated rivals who ended up working for me. See what place malice and vengeance hold in how I rule."

"Tell me." He would check, too, of course, but he liked to hear it from the woman herself.

"Vengeance only when my power is in question. Not for personal satisfaction. I don't throw away tools lightly. Especially sharp ones. If I send you after four wetboys and you kill them all, and you learn the secrets of the fifth, how could I possibly threaten you? I would rather keep you."

"A pet?"

"An ally. A lover—insofar as you don't interfere with my work or who I bed."

"You won't ever ask me to take the magical oath?"

"I don't think I'll need to." She smiled. Beautiful.

"That's not what I asked," Gaelan said.

She smiled more broadly, pleased to be matched. "I won't ever ask or compel you to take any sort of oath of obedience."

"So if I do this, what are you going to give me? Aside from piles of coin and the best love-making of my life? Which I take as a given."

She smiled again, then said, "A network of spies who will find the man you're looking for."

A fist of stone wrapped around Gaelan's chest. A long moment. He couldn't breathe. "Very well," he said finally. "Assuming everything is as you've said. I'll check, and you have this Scarred Wrable meet me at my inn tomorrow night."

She smiled. Trailed her fingers down the

lines of his abs. Lower. "One more time?" she asked.

Scarred Wrable was a lanky man of Friaki ancestry. Round-cheeked and sallow-skinned, with hair like a sheaf of black wheat and the long, lean muscles of a martial artist. He was seated in Gaelan's bed, in his locked room. The seals on the door were intact, the lock not obviously picked. Professional pride.

"Ben Wrable?" Gaelan asked. Gwinvere's story had checked out, as he had expected it would. She was ferocious when crossed, but magnanimous when she could be. Generous to the best or those she suspected could be the best. Never one to destroy what could instead serve. Liked kids.

Ben rose and two daggers popped out of nowhere, flying, hilts first.

Gaelan snatched them out of the air, unthinking.

Ben grinned recklessly. “The Night Angels favor you,” he said.

“Night Angels?” Gaelan asked. His heart dropped into his guts. The wetboy opened the window, cracking the magical seals Gaelan had put on them.

Scarred Wrable said, “Come, the Devil’s Highway awaits. Follow as well as you can. First test.”

“I still don’t understand what this has to do with the ka’kari,” the little redhead Yvor Vas says. He is a member of a secret organization called the Society of the Second Sun. They are ostensibly dedicated to studying the ka’kari. In truth, they study immortality, which they believe the ka’kari gives. They’re a loose-knit organization, though, because for all that they hope otherwise, the ka’kari-given immortality can’t be shared, and most of them suspect as much.

"The ka'kari is what brought me to Cenaria in the first place," I say.

"Looking for one? Or because the one you already have told you to come?"

I drain another flagon. Ever since I bonded the ka'kari, it takes me a lot to get drunk.

It wasn't the first time that Gaelan had traversed the rooftops of a city—both Rebus Nimble and Dav Slinker had had rocky relationships with the law. But both of those men had lived in cities with more stable construction materials. It was one thing to jump from wattle roof to wattle roof or from stone to stone, and quite another to jump from slate and bamboo to thatch to crumbling terra-cotta. Cenaria grew or mined very little of its own resources, so builders used whatever they could get.

In cities where you could trust your footing, you could move faster, take great leaps. Here,

Gaelan and Ben Wrable moved at little more than a sprint, jumping lightly and landing lightly.

Gaelan landed on a section of terra cotta that crumbled under his feet, rolled, and sprinted on.

"Good!" Ben shouted from a far rooftop. "You pass. Second test!"

Ben crossed his arms over his chest and stepped off the peaked roof he was standing on.

Gaelan leapt across the gap to the roof and ran to the spot where the wetboy had disappeared. There was nothing there. Wind. Misting rain. He searched the darkness, muscles tensed. But even his preternatural sight didn't help.

"Here," a voice whispered.

Gaelan whipped around, daggers coming out, dropping low. There was nothing where the voice had come from.

Something slammed into the back of his knee and swept him off his feet. He fell, tumbling down the steep roof. The daggers went flying as his fingertips fought for purchase on the slate tiles.

He fell off the roof. He swung his hands, expecting a gutter—some kind of edge. Nothing. There were only a few decorative dog gargoyles. He reached. Missed.

Phantom hands made of pure magic whipped out beyond his own fingers and snagged the gargoyle. He pulled so hard he ripped it right off—and threw himself back up and onto the roof.

He landed in a fighting stance, a Plangan style, almost ludicrously low, but helpful with the steep pitch of the roof here in case he had to use his hands.

But Ben Wrable was standing, arms folded, chuckling.

"Looks like you don't know everything yet, sword swinger."

"You can throw your voice," Gaelan said.

Ben smiled.

"You won't catch me like that again," Gaelan vowed.

Ben walked over to the edge, looked down at where the dog gargoyle lay shattered far below.

A crowd had gathered, alarmed, looking up. "Enough entertainment for the locals."

"Where'd you pick up this style?" Gaelan asked as they sparred the next night. Ben Wrable's style with the staff reminded him of Peerson Jules, one of the last non-crazy Lae'knaught under-lords. That had been two hundred years ago.

"Made it up," Ben said. "My own master only did bladed weapons." He grabbed a pair of sais off the wall and slowly faded from sight. Embracing the shadows, he called it. In bright light, it reduced him to a man-size smudge of inky blackness—nothing close to invisibility, nothing close to what Gaelan could do with the aid of his ka'kari—but on a dark night it was pretty damn good.

He could muffle his steps, too.

They trained with every weapon imaginable. Ben was fast, and Gaelan was a fast learner. Ben was obviously impressed with the warrior, though Gaelan tried to hide some of his more impressive skills. Ben also mentioned other wetboy skills that he himself didn't practice and gave Gaelan an enormous tome of poisons: "My master had, uh, an accident before he could teach me most of this, and I'm a bad reader."

"That's awfully generous."

"Don't worry. I'm charging Gwinvere for it."

Ah. Ben couldn't read the coded notations, so the book was worthless to him, but it wasn't the kind of thing you could fence. Who'd buy it? If someone did, they might be your enemy. Far better to charge a friend full price and make it their problem. Clever.

Ben wasn't much help with disguises, though, saying with his scars he wasn't going to pass as anything other than himself.

He watched Gaelan shoot the bow, nailing a bull's-eye ten times in a row from a hundred paces—Gaelan was justly famous for his archery—and said, "Looks like we won't need to cover that."

Gaelan couldn't master the art of throwing his voice, though. Ben could mimic voices perfectly, as well—something Gaelan was certain was akin to the more massive sorts of body magic he himself did.

Teaching Ben a few of his own tricks would have been only fair, but much as Gaelan liked Ben, the man was a stone killer. Gaelan wasn't going to teach a wetboy those abilities.

One day, two weeks in, they were fighting sickle against chain spear. They'd been working for ten hours, sweating copiously from the fire they kept going in the room to refill their Talents. Ben threw off his tunic and Gaelan saw the rest of the man's scars for the first time.

The Friaki were much more likely to scar with keloids than people of other nations: their bodies pushing scars outward, giving them a raised appearance. Ben Wrable was covered with self-inflicted keloid scars from his neck to his fingertips.

"I was a *gorathi*'s son. A prince, if you will. I

was kidnapped as a young boy from my clan. A great insult to my father. In Friaku, a son is his father's strength. I was brought here and sold into the Death Games, where I excelled. When I won my freedom, I went back to Friaku, but my clan had been massacred long ago. No one knew their names. For all I know, the slave traders lied, and I'm just a peasant's son. I'll never know."

The Friaki had a taboo against speaking about the dead. Ben might have spoken to his own uncle, and if he hadn't approached the subject just the right way, the man would have denied knowing anything. Not having been raised there, Ben wouldn't have known.

"What's that one for?" Gaelan asked. Most of the scars appeared to be gibberish. Designs interspersed with guesses at Friaki script. In the center of his chest, though, he had cut a large circle, split halfway by a single line, straight down his sternum. That scar had been cut and recut many times.

"I had a pendant, made of two iron horseshoe nails. It was taken from me when I came to train for the Death Games. I cut it into myself so I'd never forget. No one I spoke to in Friaku had seen it before. Have you?"

"No," Gaelan lied. Ben Wrable was a man cut off from a home he would never know. A man who'd been destroyed while still a child. A man trying to hold on to one small thing, driven near madness trying to hold on to his Friaki identity, because he sure as hell didn't belong anywhere else.

Besides, referents change, especially the referents of universal symbols like lines and circles. And it had been a long time since Gaelan had lived in Friaku.

But the truth was Gaelan just didn't have the heart to tell Ben what it really meant.

There is no heroism.

There is no justice.

There is no heaven.

Gaelan wasn't dressed in black. It wasn't night. He wore a plain blue tradesman's tunic and a big, worn hat, and he had his cloak draped over his lap. He was sitting on the ruined base of an old statue—long since torn down—and eating a loaf of bread and cutting sausage to go with it. The sun was going down, and this Warrens market bordering the Plith River was beginning to close for the day. A few stalls would stay open for another hour or so, hawking hot food for those heading home. But the boat shops that came and docked and sold their wares were already pushing off, not willing to spend the night docked in the crime-ridden Warrens.

It was busy, but not packed. Gaelan saw his target enter the market from the far side. He was a plain man, could have been a tradesman himself. But Gwinvere's sketch had been very good. It was the wetboy, Nils Skelling. He was reputed to be the best man alive with an axe, despite his small stature. Great climber. Fearless swimmer. Excellent in unarmed combat, said to have killed fifteen Lae'knaught Lancers with his bare hands. Said to have quite a sense of humor, too. Nils was walking along the edge of the pier. The crowd tended to be thinner there, because sometimes when the crowd suddenly swelled, those at the edge would get pushed into the sewage-befouled water.

A wetboy wasn't worried about such a thing.

There is no sixth sense.

There is no hell but life, and death is worse.

Gaelan coughed a few times, pounded his chest, and walked, still eating, cutting a piece of sausage. Among the bustling, wheezing, sniffling masses, he might as well have been invisible.

The wetboy passed between Gaelan and the water. In his eyes, Gaelan saw murder. It was enough. Gaelan slammed the knife into the man's kidney. A lethal blow, and so painful he couldn't cry out. In an instant, with the hand under his folded cloak, Gaelan clipped a lead weight to the wetboy's belt, and with a hand of magic, he propelled the man gently toward the water.

Still walking purposefully, putting distance between them, Gaelan faked another loud coughing fit to draw attention to himself as the wetboy sank to his knees, and slipped right off the pier into the water. The slight sound of him hitting the waves was covered by Gaelan's coughing. The weights dragged the body into the depths. And it was done.

There is no glory.

There is no light.

There is only victory.

"You can't tell me once you start killing," Ben Wrable said. "I'm still bound by my oath to the Shinga. If I *know* of a *direct* threat, I'll have to go report it. You understand? Not 'I'll have to do it because I'm so honorable'—it's a magical compulsion."

Clever Ben Wrable, he knew exactly the bounds of his compulsion, and with Gaelan, he was pressing right against them.

"If the Shinga orders it, I'll have to try to kill you, Gaelan. So you need to do your business before they even know it. I won't have taught you everything, but if you're successful, I can teach you the rest at our leisure. I report to the Shinga in two weeks. He doesn't always remember to do so, but if he asks if I know of any threats to him, I'll have to answer honestly."

"Fair enough." Two weeks. So the water clock was grinding away. Good. Gaelan liked to feel the press of time. It had been too long.

Like most of the wetboys, Polus Merit worshipped Nysos, the god of blood, semen, and wine. He was already half drunk when Gaelan ran into him in the brothel. He was a big man, fatter than you'd expect a wetboy to be. But then, his specialty was poisons. And claymores.

Another product of the Death Games. He'd been an apothecary who got too far into debt to the wrong people and had been forced into slavery, along with his wife and children. They hadn't made it—Gaelan knew no more than that, and didn't want to. When Polus had been pushed into the Death Games, no one thought he'd last a day. But he'd taken to it with relish. Now, he was forty-five, bald, paunchy. Still powerful under the fat, and with a massive Talent.

He took a deep drink of a Sethi red, looked down the bar at Gaelan. "You've got a dangerous look about you," Polus said.

"Bugger off. You're not my type," Gaelan said. He had seen the man's eyes. There was murder-guilt there. It was enough.

Polus scooted to a seat closer to Gaelan. "You know how other gifts sometimes come along with the Talent?"

"Hey, fuck off."

"I got a bit of prophecy. Not enough to be useful, you know. Just glimpses. My wife dead, things like that to keep me up late at night. I had this vision that I was going to be killed by forty men, all at once. Queer, huh? But now that you're here, I see they're just you. Durzo Blint."

What? That wasn't a name Gaelan had ever had. It wasn't a name he'd ever even heard.

Polus Merit chuckled quietly, drunkenly. "Don't suppose I could stop you. You know, it's foretold now and all." He grinned. "Worse times to go, I guess. My favorite girl was working tonight. She did me right. This wine could have been better, but, meh." Polus shrugged, pulled out his coin purse, put it on the bar, and waved to the server, a woman in a low-cut dress. "See this all gets to Anesha, would you?"

"You drunk, Polus?" the server asked.

He smiled at her. Shook his head.

When she left, Polus turned back to Gaelan.

"I don't ask you to make it fair. Gods know I don't deserve that. But I'd appreciate it if you make it quick."

Gaelan looked at him like he was crazy. But he felt transfixed. A Talent in prophecy. If the man started shouting everything he saw, Gaelan could be wrecked instantly. Forty men in one. Who could that be but an immortal?

"I'm going to go for a walk," Polus said. "Down along the river." He got up.

After the man left, Gaelan went out the back way quickly, in case Polus was setting up an ambush in front or in back. The man wasn't there. Gaelan made it up to the rooftops, jumping from wall to wall. He strung his longbow and checked his arrows.

True to his word, Polus Merit was walking slowly, not two blocks away, along the edge of the Plith. A quiet section where it would be easy to dispose of the body. A hundred paces away.

~You're better than this. This isn't you, Acaelus.~

It is now. Half a breath out, the blessed stillness before murder.

He released the arrow. Perfect shot, base of the skull. Instant death. Polus crumpled.

When he went to roll the body into the river, Gaelan found a note in Polus's hand. It had just two words: "Thank you."

Nigh unto seven centuries ago, there was a magical conflagration at the Fall of Trayethell, the Battle of the Black Barrow. Magic to blot out the sun, to rend the earth. Magic seen two hundred leagues away, and felt across the oceans.

It was said that on that last day, having lost friends, wife, and battle, and hope, the Emperor Jorsin Alkestes took up the two greatest magical artifacts ever made or found. He was the first and only man ever to hold both at once. With them, his magical abilities, already legendary, were amplified a thousandfold. He took in all the power of Iures and Curoch—and it killed him.

But it didn't kill him alone.

"What do you know of the ka'kari?" I ask Yvor Vas, draining my fourth ale.

"I know about them," the freckled idiot says. "Otherwise why would I be talking with you? And you know *everything* about them, so why are you asking?"

"I know what I know. What I don't know is what you *think* you know. And if you use that tone again, you'll be picking it up from the floor."

"What tone?" Yvor asks, petulant.

My fist crosses the boy's jaw. He flies off his stool and lands flat on the floor. Most satisfying.

"That tone," I say.

"You broke my fucking tooth!" the boy complains. His lips are bleeding.

"My knuckles, on the other hand, are pristine. Odd."

Hot, barely restrained rage flares in his eyes. The boy picks himself up and takes a moment to master his anger. I watch his eyes closely. Finally, he says, "There were six ka'kari. One for each of Emperor Jorsin Alkestes's Champions of Light. They were created by Jorsin's archmage, Ezra, during the Battle of Black Barrow. The Society of the Second Sun believes they confer immortality—the bearers of the ka'kari can still be killed, but if not killed, you live forever. Maybe not forever, but at least seven hundred years, which seems close enough to me. Most in the Society believe that you were originally Shrad Marden, bearer of the blue ka'kari, friend of Jorsin Alkestes."

Friend? Did you have friends, Jorsin? I thought I was one, but now I'm not so sure. "And you? What do you believe?"

"I think you were and are Eric Daadrul, the bearer of the silver ka'kari. Impervious to blades and able to form them in your hands by thought alone."

"There's a small rumor that Polus Merit might be dead," Gwinvere Kirena said. "Something about him giving a fortune to one of my girls." They were in one of her houses, in a small, well-appointed library. She was wearing a casual blue dress that still managed to accentuate her curves.

"Can you hush it up?" Gaelan asked.

"This is the kind of thing that can get worse if you try to quash it. Wetboys frequently disappear for weeks at a time. Sometimes they give money to their favorite rent girl in case they don't come back. It doesn't mean anything yet. I don't know the girl well enough to lean on her and be completely sure what she'd do. So I'd say we have four nights."

"Who's next?" Gaelan asked.

"Saron and Jade Marion."

"Two at once? Siblings?"

"Husband and wife. More than a little crazy."

"Anyone who chooses this work is crazy," Gaelan said.

"They have a seven-year-old son."

"So I'm making an orphan. Fantastic."

"They're already teaching him the business. Crazy."

"Oh, so now I'm doing him a favor?" Gaelan asked.

"In this life, some people are finished before they begin, Gaelan."

"You'll take care of him."

Her eyebrows lifted. *First you were worried for him, now you want me to kill him?*

"I mean, provide for him," Gaelan said. "You're not going to put him on the street. He gets a chance. Small as it may be."

"Done," Gwinvere said.

* * *

They were beating the boy when Gaelan arrived, landing on a neighbor's rooftop. He supposed that should have made it easier. The Marions' home, bamboo and rice paper with a steep slate roof, was in a nicer area on the southeast side of the city. The home itself was small, but had a large yard, surrounded by a high fence so their neighbors couldn't watch them train.

It was oddly careless for two wetboys, but then Gaelan supposed if you had a child, it was hard to move surreptitiously between safe houses. And any robber who accidentally came here would quickly wish he hadn't. And if someone knew he was attacking two wetboys and decided to do it anyway, he was probably powerful enough to find you regardless.

Still. Odd.

And it was the mother doing the beating. "Faster, Hubert! Pathetic. You disgust me." The boy was curled up on the ground, and she was punching him, her fist stabbing in past his blocks, efficient, crisp, remorseless.

Will you serve me in this?

~What are you doing, Acaelus?~

Serve me or abandon me, black heart. I'm going.

Gaelan leapt from the roof. There were good tactical reasons to do this—there were doubtless booby traps on the fence, on the wetboys' own roof, and at their doors—but really, he just wanted to get it over with.

Problem with jumping—you can't change course in midair. Jade screamed something just before Gaelan descended. Gaelan's sword was out, aimed squarely for Saron's back, going for the heart.

But Saron jumped instantly, and used his Talent to do so.

Gaelan's sword struck deeply enough that the blade stuck and was ripped out of his hands by the force of Saron's jump.

Gaelan hit the ground off-balance and rolled, popping to his feet and throwing a pair of knives at Jade.

She stood still, apparently stunned by his appearance.

The knives passed through her, and she *popped.*

Mirage! Of course. Jade was a master of illusions.

A door slammed. The back door of the house. Jade had already escaped.

The boy had risen. He was staring at Gaelan wide-eyed.

"Sorry, kid," Gaelan said. "Nothing to do with you." He jumped over the fence into the neighbor's much smaller yard—approximately where he thought Saron should have landed.

Saron was in the yard, standing on trembling legs, leaning against a sapling for support. Gaelan's sword had entered his back and exited below his belly button. The force of his jump had yanked it downward, but it hadn't cut all the way through his pelvis—so the blade was sticking out of his crotch, angled down. Blood dripped off the sword's point like piss dribbling off a penis.

"You won't get it," Saron said.

"Get what?" Gaelan asked, playing along.

"The red stone. The fire ruby."

The red ka'kari? What the hell? "You're dying," Gaelan said. "If you don't make your move soon, you won't have the strength."

Saron shifted, and a gush of blood and worse splurted onto the ground from his groin. A knife tumbled out of his nerveless fingers. He grunted, face contorted in pain. "Too late. Curse you."

"How much does she love you?" Gaelan asked quietly.

"What?" Saron's eyes suddenly showed a bit of real fear.

Gaelan lowered his voice further. "Because I want to know if I'm going to have to chase Jade down, or if she'll come back if I stand here talking to you long enough."

~You're despicable, Gaelan.~

Spare me.

"I'll kill you!" Saron shouted.

Raising his voice. Doubtless to cover the approach of—

Gaelan threw himself to the side.

A spear pierced the air where he'd stood a second before. A mistake. She should have attacked with projectiles. She thrust again immediately as he moved in. The blade cut his tunic as it passed between his torso and his arm.

Gaelan locked his elbow around the spear's shaft, trapping it as he twisted, bringing up his other hand and snapping the shaft below the spearhead before Jade could snatch it back.

Give her this. She'd been overcome by emotion for a moment—wanting to kill him immediately so she could tend to her dying husband—but she was cool now. She instantly lashed out again with the broken weapon, using it as a staff, unfazed.

Unarmed, Gaelan dodged behind the sapling where Saron was leaning, dying. Her strike rattled the whole tree, making Saron groan.

She stabbed at Gaelan, right past Saron. Once, twice. Gaelan dodged, dodged, then blocked, absorbing the blow and throwing her back. He ripped his sword free of Saron's back.

Jade was blonde, with appropriately green eyes, hard and skinny. A muscular beauty.

She began spinning the staff in great, fast circles, while she circled Gaelan widdershins. Saron was groaning again. He'd fallen to the ground, propped awkwardly against the little sapling.

Jade made no move to attack, her face a mask of intensity, stance low, staff whirling.

Gaelan would have been fooled if his eyes weren't so good, ka'kari aided. But there was a slight shimmer to Jade's figure. And that spinning staff made no noise as it cut the air.

Dropping low, Gaelan spun, attacking *behind* himself, his sword cutting a gleaming arc—batting aside a shadowy sword as the real Jade, shadow-cloaked, attacked from behind him.

Gaelan's lightning-fast riposte cut halfway through her neck. Jade dropped instantly. His blade had cut her spine. Arterial blood jetted over his face as his sword slid out of her neck. The shadows she'd wrapped around her body retreated. Disappeared.

The illusion of her—her distraction, her doppelganger—continued circling, whirling the phantasmal staff. Jade had split it off from herself when Gaelan had turned away to grab his sword. Then she'd wrapped herself in shadows, and had circled him the opposite way. Clever.

The illusory Jade circled all the way to Gaelan, intent on spinning her staff.

At Gaelan's touch, the illusion fell apart.

When Gaelan turned again, Jade was dead. Her illusions had outlived her.

Not so different, are we?

The Marions' little boy, Hubert, came running into the yard with a little, child-sized crossbow in his hands, crying. "Father! Father!"

Not ten paces away, wrapped in shadows, gathered in the arms of the night, Gaelan watched. With one hand, he rubbed his temples.

"Mother! Mother!" The boy, the orphan, ran to her corpse.

Darkness.

Gwinvere guided Gaelan to the basin, washed the blood off his hands. He knew he should snap out of it, but he was wooden, leaden, numb. Dead.

Jade, blond hair stained into a black halo around her head, neck cut at a sharp upward angle from collarbone to chin.

Jerissa, petite Cenarian with brown eyes, expression blank, never again to show her quirky grin, dress matted with blood from a single sword stroke through her heart.

Ysel, round Ymmuri face angelic, chest crushed, every rib snapped.

Lithel, kinky Ladeshian hair pulled into many small braids, eyes open, blackballed from the blow that had crushed the back of her skull.

Hannan, still a beauty at seventy, hair like

ivory, smile lines by the dozen. The bruise prints of strangling hands around her neck.

Direla, her dusky Sethi skin fine, nose patrician, hair almost blue-black. The violence that had killed her hadn't left any marks—at least not on her face.

Fayima, features so demolished he wouldn't have been able to recognize the young princess if not for the little mole on the side of her neck.

Platinum-blond Ahnuwk. Aelin, the fire dancer. Kir, exiled duchess turned pirate.

And on it went. A line of women, young and old. His wives and lovers from over the centuries. All dead. All dead because of him. One way or the other.

He turned and saw a line of dead children. His children. His dead. His fault.

Gwinvere pulled his tunic over his head like he was a child. He was standing beside a steaming tub of water. He hadn't even noticed it being brought in.

*　　*　　*

"You've come a long way, Tal Drakkan—or is it Gaelan Starfire now? So hard to run from the past, isn't it?" The man sat astride his fine midnight warhorse. A self-satisfied smirker. He was the kind of man you knew was headed for a fall, but not for a while.

Gaelan sneered. Said nothing. Continued walking home.

"You're a duke, not a dirt farmer. This is beneath you. You're a warrior! I want you to fight for me, Gaelan Starfire," Baron Rikku said, "and I won't take no for an answer."

"Oh yes you will."

Gaelan was working in the field, repairing his fence after the heaving and shifting of the ground in the winter, stacking the big, flat rocks back into their places while his big, shaggy aurochs looked at him quizzically.

"Sure," he told the big one he called Oren.

"Pretend you won't try to jump this soon as I turn my back."

Gaelan found one of the boulders that had slipped and rolled from its place. He looked left and right to see if any of the neighboring farmers were within sight. They already wondered how he was able to do so much of the heavy work by himself.

No one.

He grabbed the boulder and, with his Talent surging, picked it up and set it back in place.

"Not bad? Huh?" he said, slapping his hands free of dirt and mud.

Oren didn't seem impressed.

Gaelan liked being a farmer. Enough physical labor to keep him fit without the use of body magic. The imposition of order on the chaos of nature. The straight lines of plowing. The simplicity of his neighbors, who didn't ask anything of him except a helping hand once in a while for a barn raising.

He fixed a full league of fence before darkfall. And walked home, dirty, sweaty, and happy.

When he got home, on the big oak out front, he found his daughter and his pregnant wife. Hanged.

He dropped to his knees. Screamed.

"Seraene. Alinaea." The names came out as sobs.

"Shh. Shh."

Gwinvere held him in her bed, her arms around him, protective. She stroked his hair over his temples.

When he woke in the morning, Gwinvere was already up. She looked at him with what he swore was real desire in her eyes. "Take me," she said. "You'll feel like yourself again afterward."

Truth was, he *already* felt better. He'd slept the memories off like a bad batch of mushrooms. But only a fool would turn down a woman as beautiful as Gwinvere Kirena. He pulled her into his arms.

* * *

"There's only one kill left," Gwinvere said. She was in her dressing gown, her cheeks still flushed from their lovemaking, but she was abruptly all business.

Gaelan sat up in bed. "Who?"

"Scarred Wrable, Gaelan. He's the only one who knows who you are. He's the only one who can guess what I'm doing. And he's been ordered to report to the Shinga. Tonight. I'm sorry to ask you to do this, but it's the only way."

"*Arutayro?*" a voice asked next to Gaelan's table. It was an old wetboy tradition—an oath of nonaggression for one hour. The inn was dark, smoky with tobacco and riotweed. The kind of place where no one asked questions of strangers.

"*Arutayro*," Gaelan affirmed. On the table, wrapped in a sash, were all of his weapons.

Ben Wrable set his sash full of weapons on the table next to Gaelan's. He sat. "I didn't expect you to know *arutayro*, Gaelan. That's old. Real old."

"So am I."

"I doubt that. I bet I'm older than you are," Ben said.

"Hmm. How long we got?"

"I'm to report in three hours. So if you're going to try to kill me, you'll need to—"

"I'm not."

"Go on, Gaelan. Give me the dignity of honesty. I know Gwinvere. I don't take it personal. Her back's to the wall. If you let me go, the other wetboys will..." He trailed off. His eyebrows climbed. "You already got the others?"

Gaelan nodded.

Ben cursed. "Even Jade and Saron?"

"They were tough."

Ben whistled. Thinking he was being summoned, a serving man came over. "Uh, two ales," Ben said. The man left. "If you don't kill me, Gaelan, the Shinga will order me to kill *you*. You'll only push your problems back a day or two. And he'll send the bashers and all the apprentice wetboys after you."

"I lied to you about that symbol you cut into your chest," Gaelan said. "I have seen it before. It's a pictogram. Literally, it means split-head. Moron. Idiot."

Ben's face darkened, fingers twitched toward his sash. Then he laughed ruefully. "I could tell you were lying the other day when you said you'd never seen it before. By the Night Angels' balls. *Moron.* And I prove it by cutting the fucking thing into my chest over and over for fifteen years. No wonder the Friaki villagers wouldn't say what it meant. And you, you're an asshole for telling me."

Gaelan nodded, acknowledging the truth of it. Took a drink. "Then I found this," Gaelan said.

He put a pendant on the table. It was two horseshoe nails, one bent into a circle, the other piercing it most of the way. Ben's lost pendant, the very one that had been taken from him when he was put into the Death Games.

A quick sneer, like *You expect me to believe this? I told you what it looked like!* was replaced by puzzlement. Ben flipped the pendant over, looking at the scores and scratches in the iron, matching them with memories over a decade old. He looked up sharply. His voice was stricken, awed. "How did you possibly find—"

Gaelan lifted the pendant from Ben's limp hand. Suspended from the chain, the weight of the nail flipped the symbol upside down: instead of being split from the top down, the circle was split from the bottom up. Gaelan said, "You were a kid. You copied the symbol wrong, Ben. *This* symbol means split-heart: the one who's claimed half of my heart. It means beloved, favorite. It's the kind of thing a gorathi war chief would give only to his firstborn son."

He gave the pendant to the wide-eyed wetboy.

Ben put the pendant on. He threw back his ale, cursed quietly. Then he held the pendant in his palm—holding it like that, picking it up from how it naturally hung, it was inverted. That was how he would have seen it last when he was a boy, when it had been taken from him. That was how he'd gotten it wrong. He chuckled, delighted. "You are something else, Gaelan."

~I'm still surprised you didn't put contact poison on the pendant. Every time I want to give up on you, Acaelus, you do something like this.~

"I memorized that book you gave me," Gaelan said.

"What book? The poisons book? How'd you memorize the whole—how'd you even read the—Oh shit." Ben looked at his empty flagon. "You motherfucker. You took an oath! *Arutayro*—"

"Doesn't apply. The poison I used isn't lethal. It'll just knock you out for a while. In a way, I'm upholding *arutayro*, because now I don't have to kill you."

Ben weaved in his seat. "How? How'd you do it?"

"Paid someone in the kitchen to dose both.

The way I mixed it, the poison's heavier than the ale, so it mixes only in the bottom of the flagon."

"But if I hadn't finished my ale..."

"You always finish your ale, Ben."

Ben blinked, slowly, holding himself up with his elbows. "But if you don't kill me..."

Gaelan left a pile of coins on the table and nodded to the serving man. "I'll have to kill the Shinga. I know."

Ben's head slumped to the table.

Shirtless, Gaelan Starfire was arming.

On the opposite side of the room, Gwinvere Kirena was dressing.

He held up a light gray tunic mottled with black to his chest. Looked at it in the mirror. Rejected it for a black tunic mottled with gray.

She held up a fiery red dress to her chest. Looked at it in the mirror. Rejected it for a sapphire blue that was lower cut.

He strapped a pair of throwing knives to one muscular thigh.

She pulled a silk stocking up one shapely thigh.

He pulled a weapons harness around his shoulders, knotted it tight.

She took a deep breath as a servant cinched her corset.

He clipped his mask around his neck.

She clipped a jeweled necklace around hers.

He slid a knife into a wrist sheath.

She spritzed perfume on her wrist.

He looked at her in his mirror and found her looking at him in hers. He was an Angel of Death. She was a goddess.

He bowed to the mirror. "Good luck tonight, my lady."

She curtsied, face grave. "Good luck, Master Starfire." She didn't say *my lord.* But then, she wouldn't.

He jumped out the window.

* * *

Gaelan jumped across a narrow alley, landed on the peak of a crumbling inn's roof, ran across the narrow beam like an acrobat, jumped and fell six paces onto a lower, flat roof.

"I am Sa'kagé, a lord of the shadows. I claim the shadows that the Shadow may not."

The clouds broke over the city. A giant crack of thunder. Downpour.

"I am the strong arm of deliverance. I am Shadowstrider. I am the Scales of Justice. I am He-Who-Guards-Unseen. I am Shadowslayer. I am Nameless."

He jumped into one of the few standing sections of an ancient aqueduct. Quick footsteps in the rain puddling in that venerable stone waterway. Leapt.

Below, a rich carriage pulled by four horses was rattling through the streets.

"The *coranti* shall not go unpunished."

Landed on a mouldering thatch roof, had to scramble on all fours to keep from slipping off as the stuff tore apart.

"My way is hard, but I serve unbroken. In ignobility, nobility. In shame, honor. In darkness, light. I will do justice and love mercy."

The man in the carriage was one of the Nine, the Cenarian Sa'kagé's master of coin, Count Rimbold Drake. Brilliant young man, perceptive but not ambitious. He'd stumbled into his position on the Nine by his sheer competence. Gwinvere didn't believe he cared who was the Shinga. So this was mercy.

Gaelan jumped across the street directly above the carriage. He flipped and whipped a knife downward at incredible speed.

The blade punched through the carriage's roof. It quivered in the carriage seat between Count Drake's legs.

Count Drake gaped at the hole in the carriage roof, dribbling rain. The dagger was an inch from his groin. There was a note tied around the dagger's handle.

The count took the note. The words were written in a tight, angular hand: "Not A Miss."

* * *

Gaelan watched the men guarding one entrance to the Chamber of Nine. There were at least six entrances he knew, but this one was the most direct. Three of the men were simple bashers—just muscle to stop passersby from entering the wrong alley. Men good in a brawl.

Will you serve me in this?

Gaelan pulled the shadows around himself and crawled, clinging to a thatch roof, keeping a low profile.

~She's not a good woman. You must know that.~

Three archers squinted against the downpour, doing their best to protect their bowstrings under their cloaks.

No, but she's the least bad.

Two spotters stood on balconies, one studying the street, the other looking over the roofs.

~Giving power to the bad to fight the evil. A devil's bargain.~

Gaelan reached the edge of the building. Two more bashers were right underneath him. *I am a devil.*

~It was to you Jorsin Alkestes administered the Oath of the Sa'kagé, Acaelus. You could lead the Sa'kagé yourself.~

Leadership is for the idealistic and the arrogant.

It would be best if he could get in without killing anyone, but he couldn't do that alone. Not without the ka'kari's help.

~Very well, Acaelus. I shall serve.~

Gaelan felt the ka'kari form in his hand. He squeezed it and it sheathed his entire body. He dropped into the alley.

He wasn't quite invisible. Not in the rain that hit his body and gave a weird distortion to the air. But the alley was narrow. The rain came in gusts and fits as the wind blasted it periodically into the cold, damp space between the rickety buildings.

One blast threw a torrent as he walked between a torch-carrying basher and the wall.

"Herrick, you see something over there?" the basher said to another.

"No. Want to check it out?"

The basher swallowed—but went toward what he'd seen.

Gaelan was already past them. He came to the door. Rubbish was piled high in front of it to disguise what it was, but the door opened in, so the rubbish was no problem. Gaelan wrapped sound-dampening magic on the hinges and looked once more at all the men guarding it.

When no one was looking, he opened the door and slipped inside.

Inside, there was nothing but a short hall, a false wall that lay open, and a stone ladder beyond it. Gaelan got on the ladder and began sliding down.

He was almost all the way down when someone carrying a torch stepped into the stone tube and began climbing. Whoever he was, he was nimble as a monkey, climbing fast for a man with only one hand on the ladder.

Gaelan stuck one foot against the wall, then hopped, stuck the other foot to the other wall. Pushed his hands against opposite walls and flattened himself against the back of the tube. Being invisible wasn't much help if someone actually bumped into you.

The climber paused just below Gaelan, switched which hand was carrying the torch. It brought the flaming brand within inches of Gaelan's face.

But the ka'kari, true to its word, true to its nature, devoured the light, devoured the heat, turning it into its own magic, making Gaelan feel even stronger.

The climber continued on, and Gaelan slid to the bottom of the narrow tube and stepped out, invisible, into the Chamber of Nine.

The Nine's subterranean chamber was a horror and a wonder. A relic of a bygone age. It was circular, but with a ceiling so high it disappeared in darkness, giving the impression that a person inside was at the bottom of an inescapably deep pit. The floors, the walls, even the stone desks and chairs were carved with every kind of loathsome animal: rats and snakes and hydras and spiders and twisted dogs and skeletons. All glittering obsidian, sharp, cutting angles. The numerous entrances were well hidden. A crescent-shaped dais held the benches for the Nine, and over them, the Shinga's throne. The sole illumination came from an unseen oil-filled channel circling behind the Nine, casting only indirect light that plunged them all in shadow.

But their hoods were back now. Some had shed their cloaks completely, like Gwinvere. Gwinvere's beauty was sword and armor both.

Scarred Wrable had told Gaelan, "You never get to see the whole drama. When you're a wetboy, you only come in at the end."

"The fact is," a tall, fat man was saying, "I think we need to be ware of this young Gyre lord, Regnus. I don't think we can control him."

A muscular man with lots of scars and a

flattened nose—he had to be Pon Dradin, head of the Bashers—said, "I say we continue to support Bran Wesseros. If—"

"He's too martial. The Gunders—"

"Are morons," the tall, fat man said. "Every last one of them."

"Where is Scarred Wrable? I thought he was supposed to report by now," a hawkish little man said.

"Enough," the Shinga announced, standing. "I've decided."

Then his head fell off.

The ka'kari made a very sharp blade.

The Shinga's head hit the table in front of him and rolled off. His body collapsed a moment later.

Nine pairs of eyes widened. For an instant, everyone was speechless. Then the room went black.

Gaelan flipped into the center of the chamber. Some of the men shouted, but the room was warded against eavesdropping. Six recovered enough to pull alarum ropes—each of which had been cut.

Now flicking the oil channel he'd closed moments before fully open, Gaelan waited until the oil circled the entire chamber, then ignited it with a spark. Light flooded the room, astounding in its suddenness.

He stood in the middle of the chamber, ka'kari coating him in a skin, his arms folded, head down. He opened his eyes, lifted his head, shrugged the cloak off his shoulders.

The Night Angel was a vision of judgment. Big, frowning, narrowed eyes. Blank face. Mouth a slit. Skin slick. Utterly alien. Without compassion. The darkness seemed to ripple about him as if he were afire with dark flames.

The men of the Nine had reacted to their terror and surprise differently. One was hiding beneath his table, barely peering out. Pon Dradin, the Basher, was ready to fight, meaty hands folded into fists. Count Drake was seated, pensive, hands tented.

Gwinvere's eyes blazed, furious.

"I," Gaelan growled, "am Sa'kagé. It is time for a change in leadership. Any questions?"

Gaelan strode to Gwinvere. She expected him to kill her, become Shinga himself. He could see it in her face, her brave, haughty, furious face. "Gwinvere Kirena," he said. "*Shinga* Kirena." He bowed before her.

A moment later, recovering first, Count Drake bowed low in obeisance before her.

Pon Dradin moved forward, saying, "Over my dead—"

Gaelan crossed the distance between them in a blink, and punched Pon's fist so hard it shattered all the bones in the big man's hand.

"No," Gwinvere said, as the man sank back, holding his ruined fist. She was recovering already, mentally nimble as a cat. "Not over your dead body, Pon Dradin. Your services are required."

* * *

A pair of stricken bashers carried the old Shinga's body out of the chamber. A third carried his head. All looked very nervous about the figure standing cloaked in the middle of the room.

They left as quietly as they could, and shut the door behind themselves, leaving the figure alone.

Gwinvere pull back her hood. "Where *the fuck* are you?" she demanded.

Gaelan shimmered back into visibility. It was just the two of them.

"You *asshole*," she said. "I didn't need you to hand me the shadow throne! In one more day, the last piece of my plan—"

"I didn't do it for you," Gaelan said.

"What?" she snarled.

"I needed you to know I'm not a threat to you."

"So you do it by beheading my predecessor? Pretty fucking clever way to be unthreatening," Gwinvere said.

Gaelan let the storm rage right past him,

cool. "I don't want to be Shinga. I could have taken it, just now. You know it, and I needed you to know that I know it, too. This work—working for you—suits me. I want to stay, and you're the greatest danger to me. Now you know I'm a tool for you, but not a threat to you. You don't have anything I want."

Her eyes were hard. Then she flashed a sudden smile. "I wouldn't say that," she said.

He cocked an eyebrow. Of course he still wanted her body, but it seemed beneath her to mention it now. Too obvious for the subtle Gwinvere Kirena.

"I found him, Gaelan. I found out where the man who killed your family is hiding."

"And that's what took me to Chateau Shayon," I say.

"Baron Rikku was the man who hanged your wife and daughter?" Yvor Vas asks.

I stare at him. Hard.

Shit, so there were some discrepancies in the story I told him. And usually I'm such a good liar.

"Sorry." The skinny redhead gulps. I've never given an interview like this to anyone in the Society. He can't squander this opportunity. If things don't exactly match up, he'll just have to puzzle them out later. He's afraid of me, but he's ambitious, too. And too focused on the wrong things. "Can I... can I see it?"

I stare at him.

He raises his hands in surrender. "I don't mean touch it or hold it or anything. I just, you know, want to see it."

I put a platinum ball on the table, polished, lustrous, covered with spidery runes. I roll it around with a fingertip. Tiny blue streams of fire fill every rune, then I snatch it back, make it disappear into me.

His eyes are wide. "Lord Eric Daadrul. The

bearer of the Globe of Edges himself. Sir. It's such an honor to meet you."

"Mmm."

"How'd you bond it?" he asks. Like it's a throwaway question.

"Your own blood, need, and the ka'kari's element." Like it's a throwaway answer.

"Its element? How's that work with the silver ka'kari?"

"Easy. Got stabbed. Had blood, need, and metal in me all at once."

He nods, filing it away. Then his voice hardens. "I'm gonna need you to hand over that ka'kari, Lord Daadrul."

"Why?" I ask. "You've already got the red."

He blinks.

"And no man can bond two ka'kari at the same time," I say.

Yvor Vas talks. Buying time, maybe. Trying to process. "It's for my sister. She's dying. We have—had—the same disease. I bonded the red on accident and I got well. So I know it'll save her. You have no idea what I've had to do to get this far. What it's cost me. What I've done. Now hand it over. You might be impervious to blades, sir, but you'll burn like any man."

"So it's not for Gwinvere?" I say.

A quick grimace. "What do I care about some whore?"

It tells me two things. First, he knows Gwinvere. Second, she really didn't send him after the ka'kari. To learn that fact is the whole reason I told him my story, most of it true. I figured Gwinvere had to be in the Society of the Second Sun or she never would have found me in the first place, but I didn't know—and I needed to know—if she'd try to kill me for the ka'kari. Immortality is a tempting prize.

"That's really noble," I say. "Murdering someone to save your sister, I mean."

"I just listened to your story. You're the last man in the world who ought to preach to me."

~He does have a point there.~

Yvor stands and squeezes the red ka'kari in his hand. It covers his body with a slick red sheen. It burns away his clothing. He'll have to work on that.

"Fight me," he says. "I don't know how to get the ka'kari if you die while it's still inside your body."

I stand, wobble. Kids these days. "You poisoned the ale," I say. "You poisoned *the ale*?"

"Ironic, huh?"

I fucking hate irony.

He throws a fireball at me.

I bring up the black ka'kari in a shield. With a whoosh, it devours the fireball.

"That's not the Globe of Edges," he says.

"And I'm not Eric Daadrul." With a little sleight of hand, as if they're coming out of my skin, I produce five little metallic balls: blue, green, silver, white, gold. They roll uncertainly around the tabletop.

"You have all of the ka'kari?" he asks, terrified, but greedy too, not yet understanding.

"Counterfeits," I say. For just such occasions as this. I roll out my fake of the red ka'kari last.

Fear in his eyes, despite the suit of fire on his skin. Confusion. The Society only knows about six ka'kari—and what he's just seen doesn't fit any of them.

"You didn't lure me here to take my ka'kari," I tell him, sadly. "I lured you here to take yours."

A conflagration.

I'm hurled through the back wall of my safe house into the marsh surrounding it. I knew fire might be a problem. That's why I chose this place. No need to burn down the whole Warrens—not that they're much worth saving. I land calf deep in marsh mud.

The black ka'kari coats my body as Yvor comes out of the burning doorway.

Fireballs burn smoking, hissing trenches in the marsh. I dodge, flip, disappear.

He throws a fan of flames in a full circle.

A splash as I land behind him.

He whips around, throws jets of flame.

They curl around my torso, burning the night on either side of me. What hits me is mostly absorbed. The ka'kari burns blue iridescence at every joint and curve of my body as it devours the fire.

I ram two daggers deep into his chest.

The torrent of fire trails off, trickles down to nothing. His ka'kari drops into the mud, leaving him naked, mostly held up by my daggers. He looks me in the eyes and says, "I should have..."

He dies.

I let him slide off the daggers, drop into the muck. I pick up the red ka'kari from where it's hissing hot in the marsh mud.

There are no words. There is no light.

Nigh unto seven hundred years ago, there was a great fire in Trayethell. A light so bright it burned men to pillars of ash many leagues away. That fire was Jorsin Alkestes: madman, savior, king. The war was lost long before that last battle was fought. But fight he did, teeth bared, laughing, incandescent. A light so bright that the great men and women of an age flocked to him like moths to a flame, and burned.

On the last day, Jorsin Alkestes, murderer and friend, took Curoch and Iures in hand at the same time. A lesser man would fear to touch one. But he, magnificent he, he bent the Blade of Power and the Staff of Law to his will.

As krul, the twisted un-men, swarmed over the last barricades and spilled through the streets, slaughtering women armed with little more than sticks and children throwing rocks, one man fled who had never fled in his life: Acaelus Thorne, with an unwanted treasure in his hands, left the fight. Under orders. He crept like a coward, outran the krul who chased him, stood among the corpses and filth and deserters at the mouth of the pass into the Fasmeru Mountains, and looked back. The krul were a black blanket held tight over the face of the burning city.

A light bloomed from the castle's highest balcony. From a hundred points lightning cracked down. Every flying narokghul dropped from the sky, becoming a smoking, bleeding rain. The bleak clouds rolled back in an instant, as if shoved aside by giants' hands, and the light swelled ever brighter. Acaelus staggered up to a group of deserters, leaning against a granite wall at the mouth of the pass, catching their breath, weaponless, bloodied, their eyes dim, the eyes of the shamed and broken. But now those eyes reflected one sharp light. Those who had slumped now stood, curious.

Titans rushed for the castle, smashing through three-story stone houses, stone shrapnel turned into dust motes dancing in the light of a rising sun. The earth heaved upward, just once, sweeping men and krul and titans and a hundred other kinds of monsters off their feet. Even Acaelus fell. Dogs whined. It was as if the earth herself were flinging her power into this enterprise. Into Jorsin Alkestes.

And then, just as they all stood again—obliteration. Light that blinded. Light that burned. Light that boiled the bloody river. Light that purified. Light that roared.

A rushing wind filled the blindness that followed. Acaelus knew only that it felt as if his very body were afire, veins burning inside his skin. Time shattered, scattered, thrown about and blown about. He came to himself, and the first thing he saw was his own blackened skin. Smooth, burnt perfect black, like he'd been dipped in tar.

Acaelus stood, feeling curiously whole, unconscionably strong. There were pillars of ash around him. Howling winds were already blowing away the remnants of what had been men. Against the granite wall, etched by light, shadows stood. Ghosts of the men who'd been vaporized. One shadow was different. One shadow stood, one fist raised, edges perfect, outline crisp—Acaelus's shadow. The others were dim, washed out. Bleached by a flood of light that had continued even after the men who had cast them were burned away. But through all the fire, one man had stood, defiant.

The black skin retreated into his body, unbidden, leaving him naked. His clothing and even his armor had been burned away.

Acaelus looked at leagues of wasteland. Nothing stirred but what was stirred by the wind. Death had taken the throne from Jorsin. A gleaming black dome huddled where once Trayethell had stood.

~Acaelus. Mourn later. There is work to be done.~

The voice came from inside his own head. The black ka'kari. It had saved him. It had been a secret gift from Jorsin Alkestes, who had told bullheaded Acaelus Thorne to flee, to live.

But Jorsin hadn't said he meant Acaelus to live forever.

I'll come back and take it off your hands, Jorsin had promised with his roguish grin when he'd given Acaelus the treasure. The liar. He'd been wan, washed out, but his eyes burned with a fevered intensity. He'd been spending every day fighting and every night with archmage Ezra, making . . . something. Never sleeping. Working on some last-minute salvation that Acaelus only slowly came to understand wasn't coming.

Jorsin Alkestes: emperor, genius, archmage, tyrant. Jorsin Alkestes was a light so bright he left shadows standing centuries hence. The semblances of men, burned onto granite walls. And one shadow was perfect above all others. A walking, breathing shadow. A shadow as flickering as the ghosts thrown by a candle, as mutable as a king's promises. A shadow who devoured light and life.

Light *is*, but a shadow undefined becomes mere darkness. And light had been too long denied the man who had been Acaelus Thorne. He was thin, fraying, a bowlful of smoke. He was becoming undifferentiated darkness.

What if the light itself had been a lie?

* * *

Mount Tenji is the tallest mountain in Ceura. When I was a kid, people used to make pilgrimages up the mountain. It's been too cold for that for centuries. It's a volcano, but it hasn't erupted in more than a hundred years. Some smoke from time to time is all.

I reach the crater on the sixth day of climbing. I'm buried deep in many layers of coats. The wind is blowing snow everywhere.

You're good for a lot of things, I think at the black ka'kari, *but keeping me warm isn't one of them.*

~You left off part of the Oath of the Sa'kagé the other day.~

Noticed, did you?

~"Until the king returns, I shall not lay my burden down."~

I pause. *Jorsin Alkestes is dead. He's not coming back.*

~Gather the ka'kari. Bring them all together. It's time.~

Impossible.

~Impossible? For you?~

And if I'm successful? I have a fraction *of Jorsin Alkestes's power, and I'm unstoppable. He was my king, but I'm not sure he wasn't mad at the end.*

The ka'kari doesn't answer. It knows me well enough to know when I have to muddle through things on my own.

Ultimately, there is only one question: Does what you do, every day, have meaning?

Acaelus had thought his actions did, once. For centuries, he'd put his faith in Jorsin Alkestes. A long-dead king. A madman who'd sworn he would return. Even from death. A madman who'd left madness everywhere in his wake.

Acaelus had given his all. He was tired of giving. He was tired of believing. It was too much. It was finished.

~He loved you, you know. More than anyone. Do you trust your old friend?~

I stand on that windblown peak for some time.

"Not to be a god."

I toss the red ka'kari into the crater.

I strap the *schlusses* to my feet, and head down the mountain at great speed. Ordinarily, the speed and danger give me a fierce joy. But now I'm a husk. I'm like the great sequoys of Torra's Bend, leaves still green but the heart rotted out, hollow, waiting, just waiting for the storm to come along that will end it all. A mummery of life. More alone than I've ever been.

The volcano won't destroy the red, I don't think. But it does put it beyond reach. Either the red will fall only partway down, but not all the way in the magma, and it will be impossible for anyone to live long enough to grab it, or it will make it all the way down, soak up as much power as it can hold—a terrifying amount—and then release it. Over and over, as long as the earth holds fire and the ka'kari magic.

I'm halfway down the mountain when the volcano explodes.

Guess it made it.

I turn my back on the volcano as I've turned my back on my king. Fire pursues me, but emptiness can't be threatened. Emptiness holds nothing, so it holds nothing dear. Emptiness knows no fear.

The Nameless is working on his new face in Gwinvere's mirror. It's important that he do this here, so she can see it and have no doubts that the new him is really him still. But body magic hurts like a motherfucker, and he doesn't want to show her the pain. He drinks more. He's drunk, and it takes heroic amounts of alcohol to get him drunk. The black ka'kari negates poisons, for the most part—a fact Yvor Vas probably would have liked to know.

"You're not as pretty as Gaelan was," she says, finally, looking at his blond hair, thin blond beard, and pockmarked cheeks. She isn't pleased with his drunkenness, but at least she doesn't seem afraid of his abilities.

"This was my first face. My real face, you could say, if such a thing had any meaning for me." Acaelus Thorne's face. A whimsical choice, perhaps a dangerous choice, but a shadow should share some semblance with the shape that cast it.

"Handsome, before the scars. A bit grim, with them," she says.

He grunts. What looks like pockmarks actually came from the acid blood spray of a monster in that last battle, where Jorsin Alkestes died, when Trayethell fell. The mages at the time hadn't been able to heal them. Now, he doesn't want to erase that last memento of the man who may have been his friend.

From downstairs, he can hear little kids shouting, playing. Street kids, guild rats, the slave-born who have no place to go. Gwinvere takes them in sometimes. They call her Momma K. Right now, the wretches are bickering—not exactly what you hope for when you're showing kindness, but often all you get when you show kindness to those who can't afford to return it.

Gwinvere says, "The captain of the city guard has reported you dead, without reporting your name. Anyone who digs will figure out that Gaelan Starfire was killed in a fire in the Warrens. There will be some rumors that Gaelan ran afoul of the previous Shinga. Since deceased. A literal dead end."

"Very satisfying," the nameless emptiness says.

"So what's your new name?" Gwinvere asks.

"Durzo," he says into his flagon as he raises it for another drink. "Durzo Flint." He'd often carried surnames that meant something, and it seems to be a tradition among some of the wetboys as well. Flint: sharp, dangerous, brittle. Fair enough.

"Durzo Blint?" she asks, misunderstanding him.

From Flint to Blint. A portmanteau of *flint*

and *blunt*, perhaps. The sharp and the blunt. A paradox smashed together. Or just smashed. A descent from meaning to meaninglessness. It seems appropriate. He suddenly remembers Polus Merit's prophecy. Polus had said Blint, too, hadn't he? "That's right," he says. "Durzo Blint." He drinks. *Here's to you, Polus Merit. You fat pain in the ass.*

"Well, *Durzo*, I've got a job for you," Gwinvere says. "Someone who needs killing."

Gwinvere Kirena is strength incarnate. Perfection in flesh. Utterly flawless, and somehow thereby utterly sterile, impervious. When he looks at Gwinvere, he doesn't see a woman who will ever be caught off her guard. She will never be hanged, or strangled, or have her throat cut, or have her brains beaten out. She's too strong for that, too smart.

Gwinvere doesn't need him, so he can't fail her. She is the cold safety of a lean-to in the rain, not the false comfort of a stone castle that will fall on your head and destroy you utterly.

She extends a scrap of paper.

Gwinvere likes kids. An odd juxtaposition. A scrap of humanity.

This is what I get. This is what I deserve. Scraps.

He doesn't look at the paper. He doesn't take his eyes off of hers, mirroring him. He doesn't care whose name is on the note. He doesn't care what they've done. "I'll take it," he says.

I, Night Angel

The big man is tied to a tun barrel as tall as he is, with his face pressed against it, and his arms spread like a child begging for a hug. The best torture is imagination.

The barrel is lying on its side, full of wine, and it's as heavy as any ten or twelve men put together. The way Ugh's tied, he could push off from his toes and roll it—if he wanted to crush his own head when it continued rolling him down the other side. Tied with hands and feet close against the barrel, though, he can't get the leverage to do anything else.

"Ugh, I admire your courage. I was once tied up like you are now. Scary. But courage should be put in the service of good. Duchess Jadwin is a murderer and worse. Why protect her?"

"Oh, so you're the good guy now?" he asks. They're the first words he's spoken since his first *ugh* when I broke his nose and gave him that blood mustache.

"Good guy?" I ask. "Huh." I start unfolding a package on top of a hogshead barrel I upended for the purpose. We're in an empty cellar in a noblewoman's house that's under construction. It's dark in here.

I forget that I can see perfectly in darkness. I see that the darkness is there, but I simply see through it. When I've had to describe it, I've said the darkness welcomes my eyes. Nonsense has to do, sometimes, when you have to describe that which is like nothing else.

I light a single candle so Ugh can see. Whatever fear he was going to feel from being with a creature like me in the perfect darkness has already been juiced from his flesh.

Now to give his imagination some pulp for new nightmares.

He can see the torture implements laid out on the smaller barrel, barely, if he cranes his jowly head back as far as he can.

I peel off my tunic. Carefully turn it right side out. Carefully fold it. That I'm of medium height and medium build is generally an asset in my work, but it does mean big men don't find me threatening. As if something small can't kill.

People are irrational. You can't change it, so you work with it. I've been training for hours every day since I was perhaps eleven years old. It's not pride to note that I've an impressive physique.

But I don't act as if he's supposed to be impressed. He'll pretend not to be. Machismo is irrational, too. Instead, I move the hogshead forward a bit so he can see it better.

I unfold the cloths on the table to reveal a graduated hollow metal cylinder, some olive oil, a live mole trapped in an open bottle, and a length of rope.

I bow over the table, reverent. I light another candle.

"Ch'torathi sigwye h'e banath so sikamon to vathari. Vennadosh chi tomethigara. Horgathal mu tolethara. Veni, soli, fali, deachi. Vol lessara dei." I do my best to make it sound like a prayer to some dark god. It's actually the blessing Durzo Blint had spoken over me. I'd never heard the language before, and haven't heard it since, and while my memory is very sharp, it needs whetting now and again.

I sigh.

I really don't want to do this.

I bow my head again as if in prayer, tenting my hands in front of my chest. Ugh's head is cranked as far toward me as possible. He's gonna have a crick in his neck tomorrow if he keeps that up. And lives.

I dab the olive oil on my fingertips and take a deep breath, bracing myself.

~I love this part.~ the ka'kari says in my head.

Quiet.

I draw the oil in a stripe across my chest.

Steam escapes. I grunt, pursing my lips. The skin bubbles, and jet-black metal is revealed beneath torn skin.

I take deep breaths, and repeat the process on the other side. Again, hissing and bubbling. I moan to cover the lack of a sizzling sound. It takes me hours of practice to figure out a simple illusion, and so far I can only do visuals. Aural illusions would be awfully handy, and I know it can be done. Other wetboys have been famous for being able to throw their voices or even other sounds. But I can't do it. Yet.

Durzo's gone to Cenaria, and he couldn't teach me everything in the few days we had together after *what he calls the Second* Battle of Black Barrow. The only other people who might teach me anything at all would rather capture and study *me* instead.

"No, to answer your question: I'm not a good guy. A good man wouldn't do what I'm going to do tonight."

I smile at him, and as I smile, my teeth go ka'kari-black.

You give little glimpses.

Because fear is irrational, too.

I look away. "I want you to know, Ugh. I'm not here for you. But when the Night Angel is upon me, don't meet my eyes. If I look into your eyes then, I will judge you. I will see your every sin, and I will punish."

Much of the rest of this is mummery. The gibberish prayers, the illusions...but this last part is all true. Durzo once said that after holding the ka'kari for a long time, he became so sensitive he could see a lie as a man spoke it. I'm not that sensitive. Maybe I never will be. But when I see awful, awful things, I move to end them, because some monsters I will not suffer to live.

This man's lady, Trudana Jadwin, is one such.

"Has the poison started working yet?" I ask.

"Poison?" he asks.

"Didn't notice, huh?"

"You didn't... You couldn't... You never..."

"Should be a discomfort in your belly by now."

He goes silent.

I grin, flashing black metal teeth. "It's only a laxative."

"A what?"

I imagine he's heard of them, so he's wondering—of all the poisons I surely have at my disposal—why give him a laxative?

"What an odd question," I say. "Why else would I give it to you? I need room to work."

I'm not lying about the laxative—or about being good. I've known good men. Very irritating, knowing they're out there, earning their goodness day by day, by hard practice, the same way I've earned this physique. Knowing such men, I know the gulf between us: A good man wouldn't let this yellow pleasure kiss his neck at the sight of Ugh's burgeoning fear.

"The hell does that mean?!" he demands.

"You want your trousers off or on?"

"Damn you!" Anger feels so much stronger than fear. Weak men are always angry.

"Good trousers, too."

"Off, dammit. Off. Please!"

The ka'kari makes a hell of a knife. I slide a finger down each outseam, and his trousers and underclothes fall off.

He's livid that I cut them, swearing at me in words as damp with fear as his skin is with sudden sweat. Maybe he hoped I was going to untie him so he could take his trousers off. I scoot a chamber pot between his legs with my foot and step back.

It doesn't take long. The cramps wrack him, and he tries to hold back, but he makes the inevitable splattering mess. Odd thing, with the ka'kari covering me, I can't smell it.

~I was assuming you'd rather not.~ it tells me.

You assumed right.

The ka'kari's in no hurry to tell me its secrets, and I usually stumble across them like this. I had no idea it could do that. Wiping out my sense of smell? That is an odd kindness, though, isn't it?

When Ugh is done, I slosh water generously over his butt and legs.

"I'll kill you," he says. He's so flushed he's gone almost purple. Sometimes I forget how easily people get embarrassed. "I swear to all the hundred gods, I'll kill you."

Anger covering fear is acceptable, but the humiliation is threatening to push him into rage. A man enraged may charge to his own destruction if only he might wound you while killing himself. I may have miscalculated. I may have to do this after all.

I put a foot on the tun barrel, a thumb's width below his manhood. He jerks violently. More afraid of getting kicked in the stones than of demons in the dark. Ugh's an odd one. I push hard, and the barrel rolls.

His bonds lift him off his feet, and into the

air. When he's fully lying atop the tun barrel, I kick blocks beneath it to keep it from rolling farther. I adjust his bonds to draw his knees out, froglike, ass in the air.

I slosh water again on his privates, making sure he's clean.

Oh, I'm sorry, does this offend your delicate sensibilities? You know what kind of man I am. You know the work I do.

"What are you doing?" he asks, and this time the mask of anger is thin as rice paper.

~A question I was going to ask myself. Albeit for different reasons. Are you narrating*?~* the ka'kari asks.

I'm telling the story once, in my head, as I do it.

~Then later, you'll just have to write it all down?~

That's the plan.

~You think your memory is that good?~

No, no, quite the opposite. See, I do it this way because everyone's memory is bad. If I try to remember exactly what happened later, long after it's all happened, I'll... What's that word? Where you half-remember two things and put them together accidentally without realizing it?

~Confabulate.~

Right. This way, I note what happens as we go, and if I live so long, I'll write it down. If she didn't want the story in rough, she should never have asked.

~But you're not actually *writing it down as it happens.~*

No, I'm *not. Because I'm not shape-shifting metal.*

~What?~

You know your letters. You've carried written messages before. I've seen it. So you get to write down what I'm thinking aloud as we go.

~You're turning me into your scribe*?!~* He—it—swears at me then. Sometimes the ka'kari's curses are breathtaking, other times baffling. What, precisely, *is* a rump-fed runion?

It's something to worry about later. Durzo

himself warned me a hundred times—a thousand—about not getting distracted just because you think you're in control.

I say, "In Cenaria, the Sa'kagé was constrained from the top. Our Shinga had a code. She weeded out the monsters. Thought they were bad for our work. Thought they invited investigations, interference." Momma K is a singular character, and I respect her more than anyone. If anyone can successfully make the transition from crime lord to queen, it will be her. "But other cities aren't so lucky with their scum. I was visiting the Sa'kagé in—well, never mind where—and they were torturing a woman. They didn't care if she died, which is an important thing to decide when you start torturing someone. They had a method that was one of the most disturbing things I've ever seen. I'm going to see if it works on a man."

Piquing the imagination. Very important in torture.

Some inchoate cursing follows.

I dribble olive oil down his butt crack.

Oh, right, we were talking about your delicate sensibilities. You're curious about the work of a killer—and now a torturer, it turns out—but you don't want to hear anything too disgusting. Odd little bundle of contradictions you've got going there, isn't it?

But fine, I've got my own little contradictions my own self.

Damn, that didn't really sound very good, did it? Maybe I will have to edit these recollections a bit. Later. If I live that long.

Remind me to edit these, would—

~Oh fuck off.~

Anyway, I'll warn you when it's time to turn away from what I do. You can trust me. I'll let you stand at a safe distance. I won't describe the irregular mole by his hairy butthole or his shriveled scrotum.

More cursing. He flails against his bonds so hard that if I hadn't used silk rope, he'd have bloodied his ankles and wrists by now.

"I've got friends. I'm not here alone! They'll be here any moment."

Friends, he calls them. Tougher than he looks if that's the lie he tells now.

"Were there the six, or was that seventh one of them, too? I couldn't tell. He moved like a civilian, but I took him out as well. Just to be safe."

Silence. Then he says, "Dear gods."

I don't tell him, of course, but I didn't kill them. A knockout poison and a lot of rope. Dosing is a huge problem with knockout poisons. What's lethal for one person, another shakes off in an hour. Durzo figured out some of the factors that affected that: good physical condition, habitual drinking, and oddly, vegetarianism can all push sensitivity up. But when you don't have time to ascertain a deader's full dietary and chirurgical history, you make do. Rope and gags.

Like so much else in wet work, you've got to have solid fundamentals to back up the magic and the toys.

I move to the table again to draw his attention to the items there. He looks at them blankly.

This one's imagination appears to be a blunt instrument.

Fine, then.

I pick up the hollow graduated cylinder and smear oil generously on it.

Then I put it down, disgusted. That also isn't an act.

"I don't think I can do this," I say quietly. A lie. I'm capable of a great deal worse. "But *he* can."

Hints and intimations have done nothing. Time to drop subtlety completely.

I grab at my bare chest and groan. Then I start digging, as if cracking open the heavy covers of a book. As the skin peels back over my sternum, a single iridescent blue line is revealed against a black carapace. I'm still experimenting with my Night Angel physique, but I like this deep-burning cool blue. Don't know why. I might be immortal; I might live seven hundred years like my master, but right now I'm twenty. I think it's scary.

Ugh's eyes bug out.

I brace myself and tear my skin off like I'm shucking off a coat. It is pretty horrific looking, if I do say so myself. Skin clings to my hands, and at my neck and above, it's bleeding from being torn. My chest is all gleaming obsidian muscle and blue accent lines.

I walk out of the line of his sight. He turns, looking for me, but he can't turn far enough. Sweat drips down his cheeks, dampens his hair. *Finally.*

I grunt and groan, as if in more pain, but really to make noise to cover the sound of me stripping off my trousers and underclothes. The ka'kari could simply devour them—but then I'd be without trousers and underclothes.

~You're not bringing that up again, *are you?~*

I let the ka'kari come to my skin. It covers me perfectly and silently in black metal curves and—grudgingly—burning blue accents. The ka'kari seems less impressed with me than I am.

~Reminder. Edit out 'seems.'~

I keep the ka'kari free of my head, though—it'll be best to do this in stages if I don't want to actually torture Ugh.

As I step back into view, he says, "Gods, what are you?"

"Not a good guy. Not that." I'm still working on the voice. I haven't had to speak much as the Night Angel. It should sound different from my regular speaking voice, though, shouldn't it? I want to be intimidating, like the Night Angel is actually possessing me or something—like I'm not in control of my actions—but I don't want to be goofy raspy. Also, I should do the voice only when I'm wearing the entire outfit, including over my face, right?

No time to think about it now.

I say, "I aspire to be a good tool. I am the imperfect avatar of an immutable ideal. Your lady has escaped, but only for a time. War does that. The righteous perish and black deeds go unpunished. The king's amnesty was necessary for there to be healing afterward—for good men under great duress do evil—but some take advantage of war, and then they try to take advantage of peace. And of those, some do escape the king's justice—but not her. For I am the reaching hand of the curse. I am the fist of retribution. I am the hungry maw of justice. I am the sharp teeth of vengeance. I am the open throat to hell. I am the Night Angel, and I do not forgive."

I can't tell if his silence now means I have a great future as a torturer, or none.

"So." I lower my voice. "I'm going to tell you exactly what I'm going to do next, and if you're completely honest with me, I'm going to leave you a very dull knife you can use to cut your ropes and escape."

"You idiot, you fool! Release me this instant! My men are on their way even now. Don't you know who I am?"

Ah, progress.

"You are Duke Aemil Jadwin. Brother to the late duke, husband to the late duke's wife. Clearly she didn't grieve your brother's death for long. One wonders how long she'll grieve you or how much your fortune will comfort her. Aemil, you're bad with disguises, and your men don't like you much."

Of all the things, *this* finally unmoors him. Is it that I saw through his disguise that he thought so clever? Or that his men don't admire him so much as they pretend?

But I've got him on his heels, so I keep going. "I know who you are, and no one knows we're here. Because we're not where you think we are. I moved you while you were unconscious. No one's coming to save you. I'm not the best at what I do, but I am very, very good. Duke Jadwin, your wife's cheated on you already, but I don't ask you to avenge yourself on her. I care not for her sins against you. Trudana murdered the prince. A loathsome character in his own right, but his murder precipitated war. A war in which many thousands died. And then she, a traitor and murderess and, not least among her crimes, an artist, she made statues from the bodies of the dead. Including two of my friends.

"I need two things from you: the name of the mage who helped her in her work, and Trudana's location."

"What are you going to do to me?"

Imagination is the best torture. But second bests abound.

"This tube goes in your rectum. I force the mole down the tube. Then I tie your legs together so it can't get out the way it went in. The mole panics and tries to dig out some other way. Good diggers, moles, and don't need much air. Sometimes they actually dig their way out."

"Oh gods have mercy." He is right at the edge of tears, but I quash my conscience. He is not a man; he is an obstacle tripping me up as I pursue justice for my dead loved ones.

"Don't make me do it, Duke. I don't like killing the innocent."

"I'm not... I'm not entirely innocent."

"I was talking about the mole."

And without my quite meaning to call it forth, the black ka'kari comes up over my face in hues of cold, fiery blue judgment, and I stare into his eyes and *see*.

Remember that thing I said? About how I'd tell you when to turn away? Now would be a good time.

ACKNOWLEDGMENTS

Writing *Perfect Shadow* was a chance for me to experiment with a staccato, time-skipping, kinetic style that I hoped would be fitting for these characters. I also hoped it would help me fit this story into a short form. It was supposed to be a long short story. It could easily have become a novel instead. For me, *Perfect Shadow* tells about one of the bleakest times in Durzo Blint's long life. It's a story of a hero losing faith and coming to believe a lie. I wanted to tell this story, but I didn't want to spend a year or two in that heart-space. So I cheated. I wrote it as a short story. Except it refused to be a short story, and even as tightly told as I could manage, became a novella instead.

My thanks, in chronological order: first, to Bill and Yanni at Subterranean Press for taking on the novella and giving it a beautiful treatment in a limited collector's edition that sold out on the first day. (Surely in great part due to the amazing art by Raymond Swanland.)

In the olden days prior to 2007 or so, that would have been that. Regardless of interest, other readers would simply have had to wait until I had written another novella or two or a number of short stories to make a collection. A novella is too long to be published as a short story in a regular market and too short to be published alone. (Readers would have been waiting a long time, because writing *Perfect Shadow* took me months, not weeks, and that put me desperately behind on my novel schedule. In order to keep the novels coming regularly, since writing *Perfect Shadow* I haven't written any short work for publication.)

But then along came ebooks.

So my thanks to the team at Orbit who then published *Perfect Shadow* as an ebook and an audiobook.

My greatest thanks goes twice over to, well, to *you* actually. The people who take enough interest in an author to read his acknowledgments overlap significantly with those who have purchased *Perfect Shadow* in another format and with those who have requested a new physical version. Thanks for making the other versions successful enough that what you're reading now is possible, and thank you for requesting it. The number of you who have done so has been surprisingly large for what is still a short work: I know; I counted the words again, and alas, it didn't grow while I was away. I *do* think it rewards rereading, but it is . . . short.

My further thanks to those who've come to my readings. I always attempt to present something those who attend haven't read before, and at a few speaking engagements between tours

I read a rather harsh bit of a new Night Angel novel that's been banging around in my head. (I've been intending to continue in the world of Midcyru since I finished the Night Angel trilogy.) Here, I've experimented with one possible approach. Thank you for letting me play with you. I've revised it quite a lot for this volume, but those of you who listened to it then got the roughest cut. You helped me figure out what was and wasn't working. I hope it now shines. I'm not sure if "I, Night Angel" will be the first chapter of the next Night Angel novel, but it certainly helped me hone my thoughts, and it gave me a little something extra to share here.

Last, but by no means least, my thanks to my new editor, Brit Hvide, and to Tim, Anne, Alex, Ellen, Lauren, Bradley, James, Emily, and Nazia, who came up with the idea of polishing this odd shiny little stone and treating it like a gem.

I hope it brings you some joy.